## About Alex G

I am a woollyback, which means I was born and brought up in Leicestershire. I still live there with my husband, three children, two cats, one hamster and too many fish to count. I love autumn, skipping and fresh raspberries, and I hate feeling cold, anything to do with maths, and spiders.

Princess Posy galloped into my thoughts while I was taking a very bubbly bath. I just knew I couldn't pull the plug on her.

*Also by Alex Gutteridge*

WITCH WENDY WORKS HER MAGIC

PIRATE POLLY RULES THE WAVES

# Knight-in-Training

# Alex Gutteridge

Illustrated by Chambers and Dorsey

MACMILLAN CHILDREN'S BOOKS

First published 2005 by Macmillan Children's Books
a division of Macmillan Publishers Ltd
20 New Wharf Road, London N1 9RR
Basingstoke and Oxford
Associated companies throughout the world
www.panmacmillan.com

ISBN-13: 978-0-330-43471-3
ISBN-10: 0-330-43471-3

3 5 7 9 8 6 4

A CIP catalogue record for this book is available from
the British Library.

Printed and bound in Great Britain by
Mackays of Chatham plc, Kent

# Contents

*In loving memory of David, a true knight*

# Teething Trouble

# Chapter One

Princess Posy couldn't believe her luck. She was going to Knight School!

"Darling Daisy!" she giggled, throwing her arms around her horse's neck.

"Guess what? My parents have finally agreed I can train to become a Knight of the Realm."

"Are you sure they mean it?" Daisy asked.

"Oh yes," Posy replied, kissing her on the nose. "We're off to Knight School first thing in the morning. I can't wait to find out which knight in shining armour we'll be working with." She crossed her fingers. "I do hope it's Sir Darren Daring. He's a knockout."

"Absolutely," Daisy whinnied, crossing her hoofs, "and his horse, Hurricane Henry, is rather tall, dark and handsome too."

★

Posy instructed her maid to pack ten trunks. In went her prettiest dresses, her sparkliest jewels, her coolest hair-clips, and a range of ribbons and bows for Daisy's mane. The next day she kissed the King and Queen goodbye and summoned her cushiest coach. Knight School was only around the corner from the Peppermint Palace, but Posy didn't want to tire herself out.

A queue of knightlets as long as a dragon's tail curled around the edge of the courtyard.

"Hello," Posy said to the boy

standing last in the line. "I'm Princess Posy. What's your name?"

"George," he mumbled.

"What a perfect name for a knight," Posy sighed.

"Don't I know it," the boy groaned. "Why couldn't I have been called Sissy Simon or Nerdy Norbert? Why oh why do I have to be called George Goodfellow?"

"From the most famous family of knights in the land?" Daisy gasped, her jaw dropping open in amazement.

"That's right," George replied, running both hands through his spiky red hair, "but I'm just not cut out for this swashbuckling stuff."

"It *must* be in your genes," Posy said, sounding starstruck.

"I wish," George replied, glancing down at his trousers. He moved closer to Posy. "Can you keep a secret?"

Daisy pricked up her ears and clip-clopped a little closer.

"Cross my eyes and hope to dye my hair purple when I'm older," Posy said.

"I really want to be a celebrity chef," George whispered.

"That's not going to help you slay many dragons, rescue princesses or win jousting tournaments," Daisy snorted.

"Tell me about it." George sighed.

"My family have got great hopes for me. I'm expected to become a top-notch knight."

"All the girls in my family have turned into picture-perfect princesses," Posy said, patting his arm, "so I know just how you feel."

"Really?" George asked, looking a bit happier. Then his brown eyes clouded over. "I don't even like heights. The first time I climb a tower to rescue a royal recluse I'll probably have a dizzy spell."

"We'll have to hope she lives in a bungalow," Daisy neighed, quivering with laughter.

"What if it's moated?" George moaned. "I can't swim very well."

"There's bound to be a bridge," Posy replied reassuringly. "Think positively, that's my motto."

"It'll probably be guarded by a monster . . ." George said, his lips quivering.

"You'll use your sword," Posy reminded him.

"I can chop an onion faster than you can say 'damson in distress', but at the first sight of blood I feel really queasy," George confessed.

"I think he means 'damsel'," Daisy whinnied at Posy. "Damsons are small plums."

"My favourite fruit," George said, licking his lips, "and it's just the right time of year for them."

The queue shuffled forwards as the knightlets collected their armour and went to sit cross-legged on the grass.

"You must be good at something," Posy hissed.

"My pies are very popular," George said.

"Hmm," Posy murmured, putting a perfectly polished fingernail up to her lips.

"I can see why you think knighthood isn't the job for you," Daisy snorted.

"But it *is* the job for me," Posy said, straightening her tiara as they reached the front of the queue.

She squeezed George's hand.

"Don't worry," she whispered. "everything will be OK. Just wait and see."

# Chapter Two

Posy and George marched up to the long trestle table and collected their armour. A row of natty knights lounged against the wall, soaking up the September sunshine. They were all tall, young and athletic, except for one. They all wore splendid shining suits and had plush plumes in their helmets, except for one. The last

knight in the line was old and weedy-
looking. His suit was rusty, his feathers
were frayed and he was busy knitting
something very long and very green.

"What's *he* doing here?" Posy asked
George. "He looks as if he should have
hung up his spurs ages ago."

"That's Sir Tristram Limpalong,"

George explained. "He's vowed never to melt down his chain mail."

"I pity the poor knightlet who gets landed with him." Daisy shuddered. "Just look at his horse."

Beside Sir Limpalong stood the hairiest horse Posy had ever seen. He had a mishmash of a mane and a toilet brush of a tail.

"They both need a makeover," Posy giggled, "unlike Sir Darren Daring. I want to be on his team."

"Join the queue," George said. "Everyone wants to work with dashing Sir Darren – except for me, of course."

16

Posy eyed up Sir Darren. She had posters of him plastered all over her bedroom wall at the palace. He was just as she imagined. His hair was as dark as the dungeons, his shoulders were as broad as the battlements, and his eyes were as soulful as the castle ghost. Posy felt an excited flutter in her tummy as she sat down next to George.

A flunkey in full finery tripped across the grass and started to read from a long piece of parchment. Posy twiddled with her hair and fiddled with the hem of her dress as knightlets were teamed with their knights.

17

"Master George Goodfellow!" the flunkey announced in a sing-song voice. "You have the humongous honour of being trained by . . . Sir Darren Daring."

An envious gasp fluttered around the yard.

Sir Darren twizzled the corners of his moustache, straightened his breastplate and bounced over the yard towards them. George was in shock. He buried his head in his hands.

"Don't worry," Posy said, patting him on the shoulder. "I'll sort this out."

Posy looked up at Sir Darren. She beamed her most princessy smile. Sir

Darren adopted his pin-up pose.

"I think there's been a mistake," Posy
said. "Shouldn't *I* be with you?"

"I'm devastated to deny you the
opportunity." Darren twisted his lips
into a sickly smile. "But you have been
given the staggering opportunity to
work with . . ."

"Yes?" Posy said, tapping her toes impatiently.

". . . with the most hopeless knight in the history of the kingdom – Sir Tristram Limpalong."

Posy couldn't move. She watched in horror as the old knight hobbled towards her.

"It's an honour, Your Highness," Sir Tristram said, bowing low, his armour creaking like an unused door. He stayed there for ages.

"OK, you can get up now," Posy instructed.

Sir Limpalong didn't move.

"Arise!" Posy hissed.

Sir Limpalong turned his head very slowly towards her.

"I seem to be stuck," he said, smiling ruefully. "Do you think you could give me a royal hand?"

The other knights were sniggering so much they couldn't stand up straight either. Their horses were guffawing so loudly they rolled on the ground and

waggled their hoofs in the air. Posy felt
her cheeks turn as red as the rubies in
her necklace.

There was an awful scraping and grating sound as she yanked the elderly knight to an upright position.

"You need to put more oil on your joints," Posy snapped. "Come on, let's get out of here."

She picked up her armour and Sir Limpalong's ball of wool before waving to George. Then she made a dash across the courtyard, trailing the old knight behind her.

# Chapter Three

Posy marched into the stables, dumped her knight kit on the ground and picked up a bale of hay.

"My parents are behind this!" she shouted. "They don't really want me to be a knight after all. That's why they've landed me with an old rust bucket."

She chucked the bale of hay into a corner. Sir Limpalong sank down on to it, puffing harder than a dragon.

"That know-all knight, Darren Daring, must have something to do with it," he gasped. "He's always making fun of me. That's why I've been palmed off with a pampered princess."

"Excuse me," Daisy interrupted, grabbing her favourite nosebag. "It's not exactly going to do my stable cred much good being saddled with that clodhopping beast." She tossed her head towards the yard where Sir Limpalong's horse was tearing at a tuft of grass.

"If you're talking about me," the horse said, speaking with his mouth full, "my name is Hodgepodge and I think you're being rather blinkered."

Posy flung more bales of hay around the stable until she was worn out. Then she flopped next to Sir Limpalong. She smoothed her dress and folded her arms. He clutched his knitting to his chest.

"We've been well and truly stitched up," Posy groaned.

Hodgepodge trotted in and nuzzled Sir Limpalong's stubbly chin. Daisy leaned over and rubbed the top of Posy's head.

A tiny tear formed at the corner of the old knight's eye. Posy passed him her lace handkerchief.

Beads of sweat dripped from Posy's brow. Sir Limpalong handed her a square of knitting.

"I'm sorry I was rude," Posy murmured, wiping her face.

"Me too," Sir Limpalong replied, dabbing at his eyes.

"Friends?" Posy asked, holding out her hand.

"Friends," Sir Limpalong agreed, kissing Posy's pretty ring.

"You see," Hodgepodge grunted at Daisy, "things are never as bad as they seem."

The trumpet alarm call went early the next morning.

"What time is it?" Posy said, leaning over the top bunk bed.

"Time to put on your knight dress," George grinned. "Oops, I forgot, you're already wearing one of those."

"Very funny," Posy giggled. "Now what *shall* I wear?"

Posy took ages to get ready. She washed her face until it glowed, brushed her hair until it shone, and pulled on her combat clothes. She picked some sparkly, pink brooches from her jewellery box and pinned them to her chain mail. Finally she fixed some crown-shaped clips in her hair and went down to breakfast.

"You're late," Sir Limpalong growled. "You've missed the Knight's Notices."

"It's bad news," George said. "Really blood-curdlingly bad."

"Tell me the worst." Posy sighed.

"We've got five days to track down a dragon and bring back some proof that we've found one," George groaned.

"Anyone who fails is expelled from

Knight School," Sir Limpalong said, slurping his tea through his false teeth.

"It sounds tricky for a first task," Posy murmured. "Isn't there a danger we could be scorched or suffocated by smoke or . . . eaten alive?"

"Definitely." Sir Limpalong nodded.

"My mum will be pretty annoyed if my dresses are spoilt," Posy said.

"It will be such an embarrassment for my parents if I get eaten at the first hurdle," George gulped.

"Looks like we'll just have to spur each other on," Posy grinned, and marched off to find Daisy.

★

Inside the stable-yard, Daisy was furiously fluttering her eyelashes at Hurricane Henry. He sent her a withering stare. Sir Darren was preening and flexing his muscles in front of a group of awestruck knightlets. His back was as straight as the flagpole on the castle roof, his biceps were as big as cannonballs, and his teeth gleamed as whitely as the swans gliding on the moat.

Posy sighed wistfully.

"What a poser," George muttered as he sidled up beside her.

"George!" Sir Darren bellowed. "Come and meet your horse, Typhoon Tom."

The enormous beast reared up on its
hind legs, threw back its head and
neighed as loudly as it could.

"G-goodness," George stammered.

"I am honoured to belong to George
Goodfellow, the most promising
knightlet in the school," Typhoon Tom
said, landing deftly back on all four
hoofs and sweeping his noble head

towards the ground. "I am the sort of horse knights dream of, fearless in the face of danger and faster than a speeding arrow."

"This is awful," George whispered to Posy.

"What did you say?" Typhoon Tom and Sir Darren asked together.

Posy grabbed George's hand and squeezed it tightly.

"He said how awfully lucky he feels." She smiled.

Typhoon Tom jangled his bridle in delight. Sir Darren grinned and puffed out his proud chest.

"You'll be fine," Posy whispered as

she helped George into the saddle.

Sir Darren leaped up on to
Hurricane Henry.

"Hurry up!" he snapped at George.
"We don't want to let the
others get a head start.
There might not be
enough dragons to
go around
at this time
of year."

Posy gave
George a
thumbs-up
sign as
Typhoon Tom

raced through the gates at breakneck speed, kicking up a cloud of dust behind him.

Sir Limpalong was sitting on a mounting block counting his stitches.

"We ought to get a move on," Posy said. "We've only got five days to complete the task."

Sir Limpalong carried on counting.

"What are you knitting anyway?" Posy asked.

"A scarf for Daisy, of course," Sir Limpalong replied. "It can get pretty cold in the mountains at this time of year." He patted Daisy on the neck. "We don't want you catching a cold and becoming a hoarse horse."

"I think you've got a screw loose," Posy giggled.

"Several actually," Sir Limpalong agreed, "it's a side effect of the rusting rivets."

Daisy eyed up the green wool and gulped.

"That colour is so not me," she whinnied. "It won't do anything for my complexion!"

# Chapter Four

Posy longed to gallop, but Sir Limpalong wouldn't let her.

"Can't we at least trot?" Daisy wittered.

"You're such a nag," Hodgepodge moaned.

"The others will have discovered all the best dragons," Posy huffed.

"They're not sitting waiting to be

caught, you know," Sir Limpalong guffawed. "They're rather shy and lazy. Charging in at full pelt will only scare them. We need to use skill and experience."

"But when we find a dragon," Posy asked, "will we have to dodge its lashing tail, avoid its fire-breathing nostrils and use all our strength to bring it down?"

"You can if you like," Hodgepodge scoffed, rolling his eyes skywards. "Sir Limpalong and I will enjoy the show!"

"I bet Sir Darren Daring can do all that in a matter of minutes," Posy murmured.

"He's certainly good at the dodging and avoiding," Sir Limpalong said.

"That's because he's so fit and young," Posy explained. She studied the elderly knight. He didn't look as if he'd got the strength to pull down the visor on his helmet, let alone defeat a dragon.

"How old are you exactly?" she asked as politely as she could.

Sir Limpalong scratched his furrowed forehead.

"I can't remember," he said. "It might be sixty-seven or it could be seventy-six."

"Oh my wretched relatives," Posy

groaned in Daisy's ear. "How could
they do this to me?"

Posy was worried. After two days of solid searching she hadn't had a whiff of a dragon. Trees weren't torn up by their roots, smoke wasn't spiralling up into the sky, and Daisy and Hodgepodge weren't having to jump over dragon droppings.

"They'll be hiding in the mountains," Sir Limpalong explained as he sat in front of the campfire with his knitting.

"You do know we've only got another three days to find a dragon and get back to Knight School?" Posy yawned as she polished Sir Limpalong's armour and oiled its joints.

"Don't panic, Princess," Hodgepodge sighed. "The old codger knows exactly what he's doing."

Posy was too tired to argue. She drifted off to sleep to the clickety-clacking sound of knitting needles.

"Whatever happens," Daisy whispered, nibbling her ear, "I'm not wearing that scarf."

On the third day they came to a large lake. Suddenly Hodgepodge stopped and bared his teeth. Sir Darren was lurking behind a thorny bush.

"The only dragon you're likely to catch with that nincompoop knight is a *snap*dragon," Sir Darren sneered. Posy cast him a regal glare.

"Where are you going?" Sir Darren asked with a smarmy smile.

Sir Limpalong just put his finger to his lips and carried on trotting around the edge of the lake. Posy pulled Daisy to a halt next to George who was rolling out some pastry on a large rock.

"How are you getting on?" she asked.

"I could do with a flatter surface," George said without looking up.

"I mean, have you spotted any dragon signs?" Posy sighed.

"Oh, no, thank goodness," George said, grinning at her. "Sir Dashing over there thinks there's probably a

magnificent monster at the bottom of this putrid pool."

"Really?" Posy gasped. "Thanks, George. I'll go and tell Sir Limpalong."

"There could be a dragon back there," Posy puffed as she caught up with her knight.

"No chance," Sir Limpalong replied.

"How can you be sure?" Daisy said, stopping in front of Hodgepodge and blocking their way.

"Lakes with dragons in them seethe and steam," Hodgepodge replied, pushing past her. "Everyone knows that."

"I don't think Sir Darren does," Posy

said, thoughtfully chewing a strand of hair.

Hodgepodge picked his way up the mountain path. Posy scanned the horizon trying to spot dragon clues. Behind her she heard the sound of thundering hoofs and frantic shrieking. Typhoon Tom swept past at full pelt.

"Help!" George shouted.

Sir Darren Daring skidded to a trot beside Sir Limpalong.

"That boy will go far," he boasted.

"Probably right over the side of the mountain," Posy replied anxiously.

Sir Darren narrowed his eyes and stuck his long, thin nose high in the air.

He clipped Hurricane Henry with his heels.

"We know where you're heading, Sir Hopalong," he shouted over his shoulder, "and we'll easily beat you to the dragon's lair."

On the fourth day, Posy and Sir Limpalong came to a ravine spanned by a footbridge.

Sir Darren and several other knights were hovering beside it in a jittery jumble.

"Wait," Posy warned as Hodgepodge trotted gaily towards the bridge. "It could be a trap."

"Sir Brainless seems to have forgotten that dragons often hide in ravines and set fire to footbridges as you cross them," Sir Darren chortled.

Hodgepodge snorted rudely and stepped on to the wooden slats. The knightlets peeped out from behind their gauntlets as Hodgepodge and Sir Limpalong clattered and creaked to the other side. Sir Darren's mouth dropped open in amazement.

"Here we go," Daisy said through gritted teeth. "Hold on to your helmet!"

Her hoofs barely touched the wooden surface as she galloped across the bridge.

"Phew!" Posy said, once they were safely across. She patted Daisy's neck. "That was so lucky."

"Luck had nothing to do with it," Sir Limpalong grinned. "Dragons are careless beasts. When hiding in ravines they usually cause a bit of a landslide."

"Fancy Sir Darren not knowing that," Posy murmured in Daisy's ear.

"Fancy Hurricane Henry not knowing that either," Daisy replied in a puzzled voice.

# Chapter Five

They plodded up the mountain for
hours. The path became stonier and
steeper.

Posy stopped and checked her
mobile sundial.

"We're running out of time," she
fretted. "It'll be dark soon."

"Shh!"

Sir Limpalong pointed to some

chewed tree stumps. Posy felt a sudden
surge of excitement as she noticed the
terrible teeth marks in the bark. A faint
groaning made the ground beneath her
boots quiver.

Posy gripped the hilt of her sword. Sir Limpalong held up his hand.

The tip of a long, scaly tail lay across the path in front of them.

Daisy kept close to Hodgepodge as they tiptoed through the undergrowth following the tail's coils.

A large green dragon lay lethargically in front of his cave. A feeble flame flickered out of his mouth and wispy smoke trickled from his nostrils.

Posy and Sir Limpalong dismounted and studied the dragon's yellow-tinged scales and sad expression.

"Poor dragon," Posy said. "He doesn't look very well."

The dragon let out a low roar.

Posy jumped backwards and bumped into Sir Limpalong who was taking a ball of wool and knitting needle from his saddlebag.

"Thread one of your brightest

brooches on to the end of this piece of wool," he whispered.

"We're meant to be doing knight work," Daisy said scornfully, "not needlework."

Sir Limpalong walked slowly towards the dragon, a knitting needle in one hand and the strand of wool in the other. The brooch swung backwards and forwards in front of the dragon's bleary eyes.

"Oh my jingling jewels!" Posy gasped.

"He's finally flipped," Daisy murmured.

The dragon snarled and half-heartedly ruffled its scales. Then its eyelids drooped and it started to snore. Sir Limpalong raised his knitting needle high into the air.

"Don't kill it!" Posy shouted, rushing forwards.

"He's never killed anything in all of his knighthood," Hodgepodge said.

Sir Limpalong beckoned Posy to help him prise open the dragon's huge jaws. Then he wedged them open with

the knitting needle and put his head
right inside the dragon's mouth.

"Aha!" he exclaimed, his voice
echoing eerily. "Just as I thought. A
rather manky molar, probably due to
eating too many sweet princesses."

Posy widened her eyes and took a
step backwards.

"Just joking." Sir Limpalong chuckled, wiping dragon drool from his forehead. "Now, help me remove this rotten tooth. It'll make an excellent trinket for Knight School."

Sir Limpalong tied a long piece of the green wool to the troublesome tooth and Posy fixed the other end to Daisy's saddle.

"One, two, three," Posy shouted, slapping Daisy on her rump, "go!"

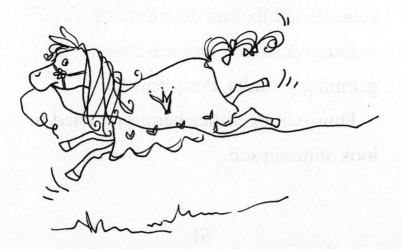

Daisy bolted and the tooth came out with a squelching, slurping sound. The dragon's scales didn't even quiver.

"You can come back now, Daisy," Posy shouted. She stroked the dragon's head. "He needs something to keep him warm."

Sir Limpalong rummaged around in his bag and pulled out Daisy's scarf.

"I've only just finished this," he said. "Daisy hasn't even had the chance to try it on. Would she mind very much if . . . ?

Daisy galloped towards them, grinning broadly. Posy frowned.

Daisy drooped her head and tried to look suitably sad.

"I'm sure I'll cope," she sighed. "You are *so* kind, Daisy," Sir Limpalong said as Posy wrapped the scarf round and round the dragon's jaw. "Besides, I can always knit you another one. I've got some lovely orange wool back at the Knight Club."

It was almost dark as Princess Posy packed the rotten tooth into her handbag.

Hodgepodge and Daisy watched

62

from a safe distance as Sir Limpalong
crept up to the dragon and clicked his
fingers. The dragon opened one eye.
Posy dragged Sir Limpalong out of
sight. The dragon opened the other eye.

Just then the ground began to thrum
like a drum, the autumn leaves spilt
from the trees and a horrible, heart-
stopping noise filled the evening air.
Suddenly Typhoon Tom burst into the
clearing and stopped dead. George
somersaulted through the air and
landed centimetres away from the
dragon's claws.

"What an emergency stop!" Typhoon
Tom boasted. "That's my best yet."

"You're dead right," George agreed,
staring up into the dragon's juddering
jaws, "and we're dead meat."

"Oops!" Typhoon Tom said, shying

away. "Perhaps it wasn't the best place to try it out."

"You could say that," Posy scolded, marching out from behind a rock, pulling Sir Limpalong with her.

"Quickly," she urged. "Hypnotize the dragon again."

Sir Limpalong fumbled in his saddlebag. The dragon stretched. He flapped his wings slightly. An ugly rumbling sound came from his tummy. Posy drew her sword.

"Oh no," the dragon grumbled, "not another knight attack."

Sir Limpalong found the wool, but the brooch was missing.

"Don't move, George," Posy instructed, fixing the dragon with her bravest glare.

"There's no point trying to help," George gulped. "It's all over for me, but you can still get back to Knight School in time. There's a pie in my rucksack. Take it home to my parents as a last gift."

"PIE!" The dragon sprang to its claws. "I *love* pie."

"I b-baked it myself," George stammered.

The dragon licked his lips with a fiery tongue. He looked deeply into George's eyes.

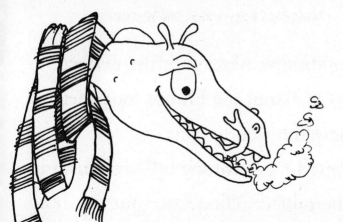

"Pretty please could you spare a piece?" he begged. "I haven't eaten anything for days because of this toothache. I'm absolutely starving."

Posy lobbed the pie towards the dragon as George edged away. Sir Limpalong was still trying to find the brooch.

"Leave that," Posy said, helping him up on to Hodgepodge. "We've got to get away."

The dragon nibbled at the perfect pastry. He smacked his lips together and kissed his curly claws.

"Superb," he swooned. "Damsons are just the perfect filling for a pie."

"If we hurry we might still make it back to Knight School before the deadline," George whispered.

"No chance," Posy said. "It's too late."

The dragon fixed Posy and George with a steady stare.

"WAIT!" he roared as Posy flung herself into the saddle.

"I don't think so," Posy said.

The dragon stomped towards them, smoke billowing from his nostrils.

"But I can give you a lift," he called.
"Don't you fancy flying Dragon
Airways back to Knight School?"

# Chapter Six

The dragon tore down the mountain
and soared into the air. Posy and
George waved goodbye to Sir
Limpalong as he led the three horses
down the perilous path. They flew right
through the night. The sun was
shimmering on the horizon as the
dragon circled high above the Knight
School.

"There's Sir Darren," Posy said, pointing to an anxious-looking knight pacing up and down on the drawbridge. "He obviously gave up looking for you and came back."

"You won't find him dawdling in dragon country," the dragon roared. "He's all huff and no puff."

"I think he must be getting his knights mixed up," Posy whispered to George.

The dragon ploughed up an entire field as he landed next to the castle.

"Are you sure you won't stop for breakfast?" Posy asked.

"Not a good idea," the dragon chortled. "The knights tend to get a bit hot under their helmets when I'm around."

"Thank you for the lift," Posy said, sliding down his helter-skelter of a tail.

"Could we have a souvenir, please? We need something to show we've met a real, live dragon."

The dragon delicately bit off the end of one of his curly claws and dropped it at Posy's feet.

"It's about time I had a pedicure," he chortled.

Posy and George watched as the dragon did a victory roll over the Peppermint Palace before heading back towards the mountain.

"Well," Posy gasped, "what did you think of that?"

George hugged the claw-clipping to his breastplate and grinned at Posy.

"It was all a bit too nail-biting for me," he sighed.

Sir Limpalong arrived back just in time for the award ceremony.

Sir Darren paraded up and down as

George collected his bronze spurs.

"Of course it helps that he's from a famous family of knights," he crowed. "Combined with my brilliant teaching, the boy just can't fail."

When it was Posy's turn, Sir Darren stamped his feet and scowled.

"I can't believe a nonsense knight and a poxy princess managed to complete that task," he jeered.

"If it makes you feel any better," Sir Limpalong said, winking at Posy, "we did have a bit of teething trouble!"

Posy led Daisy to the stables and covered her with a cashmere blanket.

"Perhaps Sir Limpalong isn't quite such an errant knight," Daisy murmured, resting her head on Posy's shoulder.

"He's certainly not a normal knight," Posy giggled, "but I'm not exactly an ordinary princess. Who knows, perhaps we'll turn out to be quite well-suited after all."

# Problem Prince

# Chapter One

Princess Posy couldn't sleep. She climbed out of her bunk bed, crept down the stairs and ran across the yard into the stables.

"Daisy!" She knelt down and blew softly into her horse's ear. "Are you awake?"

"No," Daisy groaned, keeping her eyes tightly closed.

"I'm too excited to sleep," Posy said,
shuffling closer. "Aren't you?"

"No," Daisy grumbled.

"Tomorrow we're going to find out

what our next task is," Posy said, snuggling up to Daisy's velvety-soft coat. "I can't wait."

Daisy opened one eye and looked at the inky-black sky beyond the stable door.

"Your tiara is digging into my tummy," she sighed. "I have the feeling it's going to be a long night."

As soon as the sun peeped over the horizon, Posy jumped to her feet. She raced back to the Knight School and looked in her pigeonhole. Inside was a bright pink envelope. Poking out of George's pigeonhole was a deep-purple one. Posy grabbed them both.

George was snoring gently. Posy tickled
his cheek and thrust the envelopes in
front of his sleepy eyes.

"Remember the rules, Posy," he yawned. "We're only meant to open those in front of our knights or we lose a day in which to complete the task."

"Bother!" Posy said, stamping her sequinned slipper. She tugged at George's arm. "What are you waiting for? Let's go and find them."

Sir Limpalong was nowhere to be seen, but Sir Darren was doing press-ups in the yard. Hurricane Henry trotted on the spot beside him.

George opened his envelope with shaking hands and read the instructions aloud.

**Task No. 2 (Silver Spurs Level)**
George Goodfellow and Sir Darren Daring are instructed to rescue Princess Fisticuffs from her fabulous fortress deep in Forest Fleshcreep and bring her back to Knight School within five days.

"I could do that standing on my head," Sir Darren boasted, doing just that. "Go and pack your things. Let's get set to stun Princess Fisticuffs with our skills."

"Isn't he a dream?" Posy drooled, scanning the yard for signs of Sir Limpalong. "You're so lucky."

"Princess Fisticuffs doesn't sound like a pushover to me," George murmured. "Besides, I never know what to say to girls."

"One look into Sir Darren's bold, blue eyes and she'll be Princess Putty," Posy said.

"Forest Fleshcreep sounds a bit

gruesome," George added. "I'll probably get lost and be captured by a monster."

"But you'll be with Sir Darren," Posy consoled him. "He's bound to be a marvellous map-reader and I bet he can shoo away monsters with one stern stare."

"I wonder what your task is," George said, holding Posy's envelope up to the light.

"I'm about to find out," Posy replied, pointing to a ball of orange wool that had just rolled out of the stable door. "You'd better go and get dressed before Sir Darren throws a hissy fit."

"Good luck!" George said, patting Posy on the back.

"I have a funny feeling I'm going to need it," she said, biting her bottom lip.

# Chapter Two

Sir Limpalong was sitting in the stable, knitting a new scarf for Daisy. Posy ripped open her pink envelope and read the words on the card. She felt a terrible tingling in her tiara.

Princess Posy and Sir Tristram
Limpalong are ordered to rescue
Prince Lovelorn from his Ivory
Tower high on Heartbroken Hill
and bring him back to Knight
School within five days.

"Oh no!" Posy
cried.

"Not *the* Prince
Lovelorn?" Daisy
whinnied. "He's
the most pig-
headed prince in
the whole
kingdom. Cartloads

of knightlets have tried to tempt him from his tower. They've all failed."

"I don't think I've failed," Sir Limpalong said, counting his stitches.

"That's because you've never tried," Hodgepodge reminded him.

"Haven't I?" Sir Limpalong mumbled, scratching his forehead. "Why not?"

"Probably something to do with a tower that teeters up into the clouds and a hill that has cracks and crevices wider than the most magnificent moat," Hodgepodge said. "Not to mention a pasty-faced prince who plays hard to get all the time."

"Seems like a fairly good reason to give it a miss," Daisy said, shuddering.

"Or perhaps I thought the poor chap ought to be left on his own, if that's what he wants," Sir Limpalong mused.

"I bet my parents have given this the royal seal of approval," Posy said crossly. "They never really wanted me to become a knight."

"Dastardly Sir Darren has probably had something to do with it as well," Sir Limpalong added, sagging in his suit. "He's desperate for me to retire. Apparently I don't have the right image for the Knight Club."

"For goodness' sake," Hodgepodge neighed. "You sound as if you're *both* coming apart at the seams."

"This suit of armour *is* very old," Sir Limpalong said, clanging a knitting needle against his leg iron.

"This nightdress isn't one of my best," Posy added, picking at a frayed bit of lace.

Hodgepodge and Daisy sighed at each other.

"Cheer up, Princess," Hodgepodge neighed. "All is not lost."

"Where's your pride?" Daisy asked, swishing her tail against the back of

Posy's knees. "Are you going to let a poker-faced prince prevent you from realizing your dream?"

Posy put her hands on her hips and shook out her curls.

"Absolutely not," she grinned. "Not without a fight anyway."

"I told you," Hodgepodge said to Daisy as Princess Posy and Sir Limpalong did the conga across the cobbles, "those two are definitely odds-on to become a winning team."

# Chapter Three

Posy packed her prettiest dress and favourite feather boa, some crystal hair-clips and a tin of oil for Sir Limpalong's creaking armour.

George stuffed his saddlebag with speciality sausages, fresh yeast and luxury coffee beans.

At the stables, Daisy was gazing adoringly at Hurricane Henry. Sir

Darren Daring was hopping impatiently from one foot to another. His face was as red as a royal raspberry.

"Nearly there," Sir Limpalong said, as he wound his bright-orange wool round and round Sir Darren's outstretched hands. "It's so kind of you to help me out. The wind on Heartbroken Hill can whistle more urgently than the seven dwarfs, so poor Daisy will need a scarf."

"I wasn't training to be a wool holder," Sir Darren growled through gritted teeth. "I was actually practising my t'ai chi." His eyes

swivelled towards
George. "Have you
sharpened your sword to hack
through Forest Fleshcreep?"

George nodded.

"Have you packed your strongest rope with which to climb the fabulous fortress?"

George nodded.

"Have you summoned your irresistible charm with which to bewitch Princess Fisticuffs?"

George's mouth fell open.

"Of course he has," Posy replied, polishing his helmet.

"Hitch up your breeches," Typhoon Tom advised, pawing at the ground. "I'm in the mood for trying to break my previous record for reaching Forest Fleshcreep."

"We'd better get going then,"
Sir Darren chuckled.

"Just a couple more minutes,"
Sir Limpalong murmured, "and I'll
have finished."

Sir Darren stretched his lips into an
evil grin. "So sorry," he chortled,
tossing the carefully wound wool
high up in the air above Sir
Limpalong's head. "We haven't got
time to hang around while you tie
yourself up in knots."

Sir Darren sprang up on to
Hurricane Henry and gave a pompous
wave. Then he leaned over and
whacked Typhoon Tom on the rear.

"We'll be there and back before you've even untangled yourself," Sir Darren scoffed. And they bolted out of the stable-yard so fast, Posy didn't have time to wish George good luck.

"That knight is just too big for his spurs," Hodgepodge spluttered.

"He's definitely trying to wind us up," Daisy agreed.

"Talking of being wound up," Sir Limpalong said, "do you think someone could give me a hand?"

Princess Posy and Sir Limpalong wove

through wide woods and across forgotten fields.

"We should reach the bottom of Heartbroken Hill tomorrow," Sir Limpalong said on the first evening.

"Have you ever rescued a prince before?" Posy asked, burrowing into her satin sleeping bag.

"I don't think so," he replied.

"But rescuing *princesses* must be a doddle for someone with your experience," Posy said.

"Not exactly." Sir Limpalong smiled. "Some of them can be rather headstrong."

"Surely not." Posy yawned. "Who would believe that?"

★

On the second day, Posy and Sir
Limpalong reached Forest Fleshcreep.
Sir Darren was already there,
practising cartwheels.

"I bet a knock-kneed old knight couldn't do this," he goaded.

Hodgepodge curled his lips up and flared his nostrils.

"Only a potty prince would let himself be rescued by a nitwit knight and a prissy princess," Sir Darren jeered.

Posy jumped from the saddle, took off her tiara and did hoity-toity handsprings past Sir Darren on her way to find George. He was sitting under a tree looking sorry for himself.

"Is something the matter?" she asked.

"Yes," George replied.

"Is it hugely challenging, the sort of thing that demands plenty of experience in problem-solving?"

"Mmm," George replied.

"Good! I love puzzles," Posy said, clapping her hands. "Are you worried about the dangers lurking ahead inside the freaky forest?"

"Not really," George said.

"Are you fretting about getting two black eyes from Princess Fisticuffs?" Posy asked.

"Sort of," George mumbled, "but this is even more worrying than that."

"Is it the haunting fear of falling from her fabulous fortress and injuring more than your pride?" Posy probed.

"I hadn't thought of that one," George said.

"What is it then?" Posy pleaded.

"I can't think what to cook with these sausages," George said. "It's got to be something tummy-tempting and tastebud-tickling."

"George," Posy sighed, "you should be planning your fight through the forest and discussing with Sir Darren the best way to win over Princess Fisticuffs."

"I suppose you're right," George said, "but he's been dithering about for ages and you can't carry out a rescue on an empty stomach."

★

Posy caught up with Sir Limpalong as he skirted the edge of the forest.

"Is the Ivory Tower too tall to climb?" Posy asked.

"Definitely," Sir Limpalong replied.

"Do we have a plan to get Prince Lovelorn out?" Posy asked.

Sir Limpalong shook his head.

"I find plans don't work when there are dragons and princesses involved," he explained.

"You could leave this up to me?" Posy suggested perkily. "Princesses have a knack of getting what they want."

"Is that so?" Sir Limpalong said with a smile. "Well, I've just got one rescuing ritual to perform. After that, Prince Lovelorn is all yours."

"Cool!" Princess Posy cried and she blew Sir Limpalong a lip-smacking kiss.

# Chapter Four

Early on the third morning, Posy and Sir Limpalong thundered up Heartbroken Hill at full tilt. The ground was covered in deep, wide cracks and the wind blew as fiercely as the royal trumpeters.

"Bravo!" Sir Limpalong cheered every time Hodgepodge cleared a crevice.

Daisy shook her shiny mane and raced after them.

"Hurray!" Posy laughed whenever Daisy's hoofs left the ground to fly over the gaps. "This is what I thought being a knight would be like."

★

Posy looked up at the Ivory Tower. Sir Limpalong slid from his horse, swigged some water from his flask and gargled. He threw back his head and began to sing. Birds rose out of the trees in the forest below, rabbits raced for their burrows and Posy put her hands over Daisy's delicate ears.

"Why is he making that terrible racket?" she shouted at Hodgepodge.

"It's traditional to serenade a princess before rescuing her," Hodgepodge explained. "It's only polite to do the same for a prince."

"How many princesses has he

rescued?" Posy asked.

"Hundreds," Hodgepodge whinnied in her ear reassuringly.

"When does the singing stop?" she said, wincing.

"As soon as the princess comes down from the tower," Hodgepodge shouted, munching at some grass. "It doesn't usually take long."

Posy grimaced.

"I can see why," she said.

An hour later, Sir Limpalong had almost lost his voice and there was no sign of Prince Lovelorn.

Posy marched up and poked Sir

Limpalong in the breastplate.

"It's not working," she yelled. "Why don't I have a go?"

Sir Limpalong collapsed in a heap and nodded.

Posy looked up at the small, high window. It was tightly closed. She cupped her hands around her mouth and bellowed.

"Oi! Prince Lovelorn," she shrieked in a very unprincessy way. "Give us a break and let us rescue you. Our eardrums are being tortured down here."

A sickly face pressed itself to the glass. The window creaked open.

"See!" Posy said to the others. "It's worked."

"How many times do I have to tell people?" Prince Lovelorn called down wearily. "I DON'T WANT TO BE RESCUED." And, with that, he slammed the window so hard that Posy thought the glass might fall out.

"Well, really," Daisy brayed, "I thought princes were meant to have some manners."

Posy tried the door handle. It was locked. She threw a stone at the window. It bounced off and hit Sir Limpalong on the helmet.

Posy changed into her daintiest dress and put on her trendiest tiara. She twirled and swirled all around the Ivory Tower. Sir Limpalong picked up his knitting. "Do you know who I am?" Posy shouted poutily up at the prince. The window opened slightly.

"Who are you?" Prince Lovelorn asked.

"*I* am Princess Posy, and I'm training to become a Knight of the Realm."

"You smell nice," Prince Lovelorn said, sniffing the air. "Is it a new type of perfume?"

"I think I'm wearing luscious lavender today," Posy said, holding her wrist up to her nose.

"Nah!" the prince said. "It's a nicer smell than that, more like a whiff of freshly ground coffee."

"That's not me!" Posy said. "That'll be George. He's always

121

brewing up something."

"Not George Goodfellow," Prince Lovelorn asked, "from the most famous family of knights in the land?"

"That's him," Posy replied.

"Why hasn't *he* been sent to rescue me?" Prince Lovelorn asked sulkily. "I've got a terrible reputation, you know. They might at least have sent someone good to try and get me out of here." And he banged the window shut so hard that Posy felt the ground tremble beneath her feet.

"Well," Daisy gasped, eyeing Posy's sword. "If I were you I'd seriously think about cutting that prince down to size."

By the fourth day, Posy's patience was wearing thin.

"Please, please come down," she begged. "Take pity on a desperate princess. If I don't take you back to Knight School I won't get my silver spurs and I'll be expelled."

"Tough!" Prince Lovelorn said. He leaned out of the window a little further. "What's that wafting up the hill? It smells delicious."

Posy whipped her perfume bottle from her pocket and sprayed a cloud of scent.

"I'm wearing regal rose today," she said, "made with petals picked from the palace garden."

"Nah!" the prince wrinkled up his nose. "It's not that poncy smell. It's more like a hint of fresh bread."

"That'll be George again," Princess Posy snapped, "with another of his half-baked ideas."

"Yummy!" the prince drooled as Posy stomped over to Sir Limpalong.

"It's impossible," she fumed. "What are we going to do?"

Sir Limpalong rubbed a bleary eye and stretched his legs.

"He *must* be lonely up there," Posy

continued, "with no one to talk to."

"I can hear you," Prince Lovelorn taunted.

Posy stuck her tongue out as far as it would go.

"Actually I like being lonely," the prince yelled. "I can't stand being surrounded by princesses who won't stop prattling on and on."

"I know the feeling," Sir Limpalong sympathized. "All you want is a bit of peace and quiet."

"Exactly," the prince agreed.

"You're not helping," Posy hissed at the old knight. "We're running out of time." She checked her mobile sundial. "If we don't get him back to Knight School by sunset tomorrow I can kiss my dream of becoming a knight goodbye forever."

"Sorry," Sir Limpalong replied. "I must try harder."

"That's another thing," the prince shouted. "Princesses are so bossy. Always telling you what to do, who to see, what not to wear. It makes me mad."

"Me too," Sir Limpalong agreed, checking his knitting. Posy banged her hand against her head.

"At last!" the prince cheered. "Someone who understands!" He leaned even further out of the window. "What are you making?"

"A scarf for Daisy," Sir Limpalong replied, "but I'm nearly out of wool." He gave an exaggerated shiver and chattered his false teeth together. "It's getting pretty chilly out here. Poor Daisy could catch a terrible cold without one of my special scarves."

"Oh dear, I do wish I could help," the prince said.

Posy looked up. She jumped to her feet and pressed her palms together.

128

"I don't suppose you've got a spinning wheel up there have you?" she called sweetly. "All the trendiest towers are meant to have them."

Daisy tossed her mane.

"Spinning wheels?" she neighed scornfully. "You've been reading too many fairy stories."

"Actually I have got one," the prince said. "It's covered in cobwebs, but it should still work. If you collect some wool from those sheep down there on the hill, I could have a go at spinning it for you."

"Splendid idea," Sir Limpalong grinned. "Posy will fetch it for you."

"I don't remember wool-gathering being in the *Knightlet Training Manual*," Posy grumbled.

"Neither do I," Sir Limpalong whispered in her ear, "but this could be a way to persuade the prince to come down from his tower and it will all be thanks to you."

Posy was not happy. She was meant to be doing brave deeds, not picking clumps of wool out of prickly hedges. Daisy was even crosser.

"If Hurricane Henry spots me wearing that knitted thing he'll never look at me again," Daisy groaned as she trailed after Posy. "Orange is so last season."

# Chapter Five

As dawn broke on the fifth day, Sir Limpalong stuffed the last wads of wool into Posy's sleeping bag and tied it to a piece of old rope dangling down from the window.

"We could come up and help you," Posy suggested as Prince Lovelorn hauled the bag up the side of the tower. She stared into the distance, where other knightlets were making their way back to the castle, grateful princesses smothering them with kisses. "All you need to do is open the door."

"Oh no, I can't do that," Prince Lovelorn said.

"Besides, I've almost finished."

"At least let me come up and fetch the spun wool," Posy said, flashing him a cheesy grin. "Your arms must be aching from all that work. Just turn the key in the lock and I'll be there."

"Nice try," the prince said, leaning out of the tower and lobbing several balls of wool towards Sir Limpalong, "but it won't work." He sniffed loudly. "Aah! That is the best smell in the whole world. Sizzling sausages enhanced by a sprinkling of herbs, accompanied by some wild mushrooms, if I'm not mistaken. The perfect breakfast."

"Can't you think about anything except food?" Posy said crossly. "Don't you feel the least bit guilty that I won't get my silver spurs?" Her lower lip wobbled. "I'll be thrown out of Knight School and Sir Limpalong and Hodgepodge will be put out to grass."

"I *am* sorry," Prince Lovelorn said, throwing his hands in the air, "but I can't help it."

"I give up," Posy sobbed, flouncing over to Daisy and burying her face in her mane.

Sir Limpalong cast off his stitches and held up the completed scarf with a flourish.

"What do you think?" he called up to Prince Lovelorn.

"Very smart," the prince said, giving the thumbs–up sign. "It matches my hair."

"You've worked so hard," Sir Limpalong said, "spinning through the night so that Daisy can have her scarf. Why don't you give it to her?" He quickly clamped his hand over Daisy's mouth. "I'm sure she would be honoured."

"See that," Hodgepodge whispered to Posy. "That's brilliant tactics. Your dreadful Sir Darren couldn't have invented a ploy like that."

The prince hesitated. Daisy nibbled Sir Limpalong's palm.

"I'm sorry but I really can't come down." The prince blushed bright red.

"What *is* your problem?" Posy asked gently. "You can tell us."

"Promise you won't reveal this to anyone?" the prince gulped.

"Knightlet's honour," Posy said seriously.

"I've lost the key," Prince Lovelorn whispered. "Even if I wanted to come out, I can't."

"Is that all?" Posy sighed. "I can get you out of there in a jiffy."

"You can?" the prince gasped.

"Are you sure?" Sir Limpalong asked, wrinkling his forehead.

"Of course," Posy giggled, taking the pink crystal clip from her hair.

"I'm always having to pick the lock
to the palace safe. Whenever my
mum wants the crown jewels she can
never remember
where she's put
the key. This
should be a
doddle
compared
to that!"

Posy knelt by the old wooden door while Sir Limpalong squirted some oil into the lock. She pushed the hair-clip into the hole and began to twiddle and fiddle. Everyone held their breath. At last there was a definite click as the lock sprang back.

"Easy-peasy," she giggled, pushing the door open. "See – even princesses have their uses occasionally."

# Chapter Six

Prince Lovelorn stepped out into the fresh air and did up the buttons on his dusty velvet jacket.

"You're right. It is a bit nippy out here," he said.

"What you need is something to keep you warm," Sir Limpalong suggested.

"How about a nice long scarf?"

Daisy said quickly.

"Oh, Daisy," Sir Limpalong sighed, "you are such a kind-hearted horse. Can you bear to let Prince Lovelorn have your new scarf?"

"Of course, I'm gutted to part with it," Daisy said, trying to look desperately downcast, "but there's nothing worse than a poorly prince."

Posy wrapped the scarf around Prince Lovelorn until he was completely swaddled.

"How long is it since you came out of that tower?" Posy asked. "Years I expect," she carried on without waiting for Prince Lovelorn to answer. "There must be so many things you want to do, so many places you'd like to see."

Suddenly, Posy swept the prince off his feet and bundled him on to Daisy's back.

"I know! I'll take you on a guided tour of the Peppermint Palace," she said, springing into the saddle. "We've got all these new state-of-the-art spinning wheels in the West Tower."

"I–I'm not s-sure—" the prince stammered.

In the distance they heard the thunder of hoofs. At the bottom of the hill Typhoon Tom was bolting towards the castle with George's arms wrapped tightly around his neck. Sitting behind him was a feisty-looking princess.

"Isn't that George Goodfellow," Prince Lovelorn asked, "and the famous Princess Fisticuffs? Fancy having managed to get her out of the fabulous fortress."

"Oh, George is brilliant!" Posy gushed. "And I'm sure you and

Princess Fisticuffs have a lot in common. Let's see if we can catch them up."

"D-do I have a choice?" Prince Lovelorn asked.

"I'm afraid not," Sir Limpalong chuckled. "It appears, young man, that you have been prince-napped!"

Daisy and Hodgepodge hared down Heartbroken Hill, flew past Forest Fleshcreep and pounded over the potholed paths back to Knight School. Sir Darren was lurking by the keep, longing to pull up the drawbridge.

"Phew!" Posy gasped as darkness fell. "That was close."

"Pah!" Sir Darren spat sulkily. "Another couple of minutes and you'd have been too late."

Posy jumped down from Daisy and hugged George.

"You are *so* brave," she said. "Did you charge into the fabulous fortress

146

and bring Princess Fisticuffs out kicking and screaming?"

"No, thank goodness," George replied.

"What about Forest Fleshcreep?" Posy asked.

"Wasn't it blood-curdlingly scary, echoing with ghostly sounds and with traps lurking behind every tree trunk?"

"I don't know," George replied. "We never went in there. Between you and me, I think Sir Darren got cold boots."

Posy looked puzzled.

"How did you get Princess Fisticuffs out then?" she asked.

"Just used my loaf," George grinned. "I thought she might be rather hungry after being holed up for ages, so I built the campfire upwind of the castle to be sure the

148

smell of food drifted through the trees. By the time my special sausages were sizzling, the princess was flying out of the forest and towards my frying pan!"

"It looks as if she's found a new friend too," Posy giggled as Princess Fisticuffs enveloped Prince Lovelorn in a heavyweight hug.

Sir Darren did a little jig as George collected his silver spurs.

"Of course, it helps that he's got knighthood in his genes," he whooped. "George is a natural-born knight, but it's knowing how to use the skills," Sir Darren crowed, bowing and blowing kisses to the applauding knightlets. "That's where I come in, of course."

When it was Posy's turn, Sir Darren booed and waggled his fingers against his ears.

"Is that really Prince Lovelorn?" he scoffed. "How on earth did a crinkly, wrinkly knight and a prima-donna

princess manage to pull that off? It's unbelievable."

"If it makes you feel any better," Sir Limpalong replied, tweaking Posy's tiara, "we did lose the thread at one point."

Posy led Daisy to the water trough and draped her favourite feather boa around her horse's neck.

"That Sir Limpalong is cleverer than he looks," Daisy mused, admiring her reflection in the water.

"There's certainly more to him than meets the eye," Posy agreed, nestling her cheek next to Daisy's. "But then I'm not exactly a run-of-the-mill princess, am I?" she smiled.

# Jousting with Jellies

# Chapter One

Princess Posy could only think about one thing. She was nearly a knight.

"I've only got to complete one more task before I get my golden spurs," she sighed, dragging a bejewelled brush through Daisy's tangled mane.

"Ouch!" Daisy neighed. "Will you watch what you're doing. That's my

crowning glory you're wrenching
from its roots."

"I'm sorry," Posy said. "I just can't
wait to find out what my next
mission is."

"If I tell you," Daisy whispered,

"will you give the grooming a rest? At this rate I'm going to be bald and Hurricane Henry will shy away from me."

Posy hopped up and down and clasped her hands together.

"Daisy!" she begged. "If you know something, please say so."

Daisy cast a sly glance around the stable and led Posy into a corner.

"It's been the talk of the yard," she whinnied softly. "I'll be in terrible trouble if anyone finds out I blabbed."

"I won't let on," Posy promised. "I swear on my wardrobe full of designer dresses."

"Well," Daisy said slowly, "there's going to be a knockout jousting tournament in front of the King and Queen and all the other parents."

"Oh!" Posy gasped, pointing the hairbrush like a jousting pole. "That's my favourite thing in the whole kingdom!"

She kissed Daisy on the nose and pirouetted around the stable until she collapsed in a dizzy

heap. "That will certainly weed out the weaklings," she giggled.

"Mmm," Daisy swooned. "I can't wait to see Hurricane Henry in all his finery. It makes my fetlocks fluttery just thinking about him."

"Daiseee," Posy weedled, "you are such a honeybunch of a horse."

"What do you want now?" Daisy sighed.

"*Please* can I tell George the good news? Only George. No one else."

"Go on then," Daisy murmured. "What would you do without me, hey?"

★

George was pacing up and down on the battlements. He chewed the end of his quill and jotted down a shopping list.

"Do you think I'll need extra icing sugar or not?" he asked as Posy skipped up the stone steps.

She snatched the piece of paper from his fingers and flung it into the air.

"Forget about food for once," she said. "I've found out what the next task is. It's a jousting tournament."

"Oh no," George groaned. "All that charging about is just not me."

"But tournaments are *so* exciting," Posy said. "Think of all those flags blowing in the breeze, music drifting in the air and, of course, there's always a fabulous feast at the end."

"Really?" George said, looking a little brighter. "Mind you, knowing me I'll make a complete hash of the jousting."

"Nonsense," Posy said. "It'll be a piece of cake." She peered into the yard below, where Sir Darren was studying his reflection in a water trough. "Sir Dashing down there is bound to show you how to put on a flawless performance."

Posy frowned suddenly. She couldn't imagine Sir Limpalong lifting a jousting pole, let alone fighting with it. Maybe this wasn't going to be quite as straightforward as she had first thought.

# Chapter Two

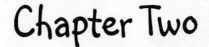

Posy and George filed into the Great
Hall for assembly.

The knights stood in a superior line
at the front, all except Sir Limpalong.
He was leaning so much that Posy
feared he would fall over.

"Quiet, please." A sharp-nosed man
in a velvet suit paced up and down in
front of the remaining knightlets.

"This is your third and final task. You will each take part in a magnificent jousting tournament. The winners of each competition will be the ones to collect their golden spurs and become Knights of the Realm."

Gasps rose to the rafters. Posy grabbed George's hand.

"Marks will be given for style, skill and splendour," the announcer carried on. He looked down his nose at the knightlets. "I will now read out the name of your opponent."

Posy squeezed her eyes tightly shut and held her breath. All around there was whispering and groaning as the knightlets were paired up. At last it was Posy's turn.

"Princess Posy is to joust against . . . George Goodfellow."

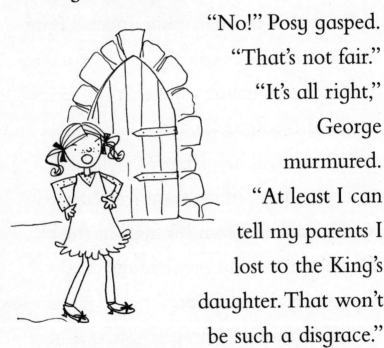

"No!" Posy gasped. "That's not fair."

"It's all right," George murmured. "At least I can tell my parents I lost to the King's daughter. That won't be such a disgrace."

"But I don't want you to lose," Posy said. "Your family will be furious."

"You'll be doing me a favour," George said, shrugging. "Once they see how hopeless I am on a horse, perhaps they'll finally let me become a chef."

"I don't want you to go away," Posy said quietly, but George didn't hear. He was busy scribbling down a new recipe on the back of his hand.

Princess Posy lay awake all night.

"What am I going to do?" she asked Daisy at breakfast time. "I can't fight George. He's my friend."

"What are the choices?" Daisy asked, lifting her head from her trough full of choc-chip oat-flakes.

"I could fight George and win," Posy said, "in which case I get my golden spurs . . ."

"And you'll become the prettiest knight the kingdom has ever known," Daisy said, "and Hurricane Henry will be overwhelmed by my grace and bravery." She whinnied, rearing up on her hind legs and doing a little tap dance.

"Sir Limpalong will remain a Knight of the Realm and George will be able to go off and become a famous chef." Posy clapped. Suddenly she became serious. "But this isn't a fairy tale," she said. "George's parents will be so cross with him if he loses."

"But if *you* lose," Daisy reminded her, "you'll have to go back to being a perfect princess and Sir Limpalong will lose his job."

"Oh, Daisy!" Posy cried. "This is a right royal muddle."

Sir Limpalong was sitting on the grass, knitting. Posy flopped down next to him.

"You do realize it's a plot?" she said, plucking at some daisies.

"It could just be a coincidence," Sir Limpalong said.

"Don't try to pull the wool over my eyes." Posy sighed. "I know my parents are behind all this."

"It's probably more to do with Sir

Darren Daring. He's desperate to send me off to the Knightmare Retirement Home and he knows jousting isn't my strong point."

"Isn't there any other way to gain my golden spurs?" Posy asked.

Sir Limpalong shook his head.

"Perhaps everyone is right after all," he said, clicking away with his knitting needles. "Perhaps I am past my prime. Maybe it's time to pack it all in."

"But you're the noblest of knights," Posy said, putting a daisy chain around his neck.

"And the wisest," Hodgepodge neighed.

"Anyway," Posy chided, "I've spent ages polishing your armour. It's just starting to get its shine back. You can't stop wearing it now."

Sir Darren Daring was strutting around the yard, waving a personalized jousting pole. Hurricane Henry was practising his sidesteps.

"This will sort the professionals from the princesses." Sir Darren grinned when he saw Posy. "My George hasn't got a rickety old wrinkly trying to teach him."

"There's more to jousting than being athletic and sharp-eyed," Posy replied.

"Like what?" Sir Darren laughed.

"Experience," Posy said confidently. "You can't deny Sir Limpalong has years and years and years of that."

Sir Darren's eyes turned all goggly. He threw back his handsome head and flung out his arms.

"Get real, Princess!" he scoffed. "You don't stand a chance of beating George

Goodfellow. His ancestors have been winning jousting tournaments for generations."

"And princesses have been practising getting their own way for even longer," Posy said, stamping her foot, "so you needn't write *me* off just yet!"

# Chapter Three

It was time for Posy's first jousting lesson. Sir Limpalong was extracting a new ball of blue wool from his saddlebag.

"Let's get to work," Posy commanded in her most regal voice. "We haven't got much time to train. The jousting tournament is on Saturday. That's only three days away."

"Don't remind me," Sir Limpalong groaned. "That's barely enough time to knit a heraldic blanket for Daisy. It has to be brilliant blue and embroidered with the royal coat of arms."

Daisy shook her head. "Not in a million trots," she mouthed to Posy, "am I wearing that thing."

Several knightlets were already practising in the yard. George was struggling to sit astride Typhoon Tom while holding on to a gigantic jousting pole.

"I'll never get the hang of this," he hissed as Posy went past.

"Give it time," she said, ducking to avoid having her head knocked off.

Sir Limpalong found a quiet spot in the corner. Posy picked up an old jousting pole that was propped up against the wall. It was heavier than she expected. She put it down again.

"Have you done any jousting recently?" she asked Sir Limpalong.

He scratched his head. "When was the last jousting tournament that I took part in?" he asked Hodgepodge. "Was it twenty or thirty years ago?"

Hodgepodge gazed at the sky and shrugged.

"But you can remember what to do?" Posy asked nervously.

Sir Limpalong screwed up his eyes and pursed his lips.

"Sort of," he said, struggling to pick up the jousting pole. His cheeks turned pink and he started to huff and puff as he lifted the pole above his head.

"Remembering is one thing, actually doing it is another," he gasped, dropping the pole to the ground with a clunk.

Posy gazed around the yard.
Everywhere she looked knightlets were
falling off their horses and jabbing
each other in the eye with their
jousting poles.

"I think we ought to start off small,"
she muttered. "That might make things
easier for both of us."

Posy leaned over and pulled Sir
Limpalong's extra-large knitting
needles from his saddlebag.

"These will do nicely," she laughed.

"Have you gone completely mad?"
Daisy cringed. "I shall be a laughing
stock in the stables."

"Sir Darren will never let me live

this down," Sir Limpalong said, shaking his head.

Posy took a deep breath and tried to stay calm.

"The way you handled that dragon was very impressive," she told Sir Limpalong, "and between us we made a great job of getting the pesky prince down from his tower, but this jousting thing is obviously harder than it looks, even for a knowledgeable knight and a talented princess." She patted Sir Limpalong's shoulder. "Trust me?"

Sir Limpalong reluctantly took one of his needles.

"Methinks Her Headstrong Highness

might just be on to something,"
Hodgepodge neighed, winking at Posy.

Hodgepodge and Daisy walked
backwards and forwards, backwards
and forwards, as Sir Limpalong and
Posy crossed knitting needles.

"I'm so embarrassed," Daisy snorted,
"even my hoofs are blushing."

Posy felt dozens of eyes watching her. Sir Darren Daring was laughing so much he had to hang on to Hurricane Henry's mane to stop himself falling off.

"Has anyone told you, you look a right pair of nits," he guffawed. "I don't think you've got much to worry about there, George."

All the knights and their knightlets rocked backwards and forwards, shrieking with laughter.

"This is tragic," Daisy wailed. "I'd rather be pulling the royal dustcart than doing this."

"Suddenly the Knightmare

Retirement Home doesn't seem so bad," Sir Limpalong moaned.

"Oh, don't take any notice of them," Posy ordered. "They're only trying to needle us."

By the second day, Posy thought they were ready to use something bigger.

"Where are those walking sticks you use when your knees seize up?" she asked Sir Limpalong.

Daisy slumped forwards.

"That's it!" she whinnied. "My reputation is now in total tatters."

"Join the club," Sir Limpalong grumbled.

"We're not going to win if you don't make more of an effort," Posy scolded.

"What's the point?" Sir Limpalong sighed.

Posy put her hands on her hips and jutted out her chin.

"The point is that you want to stay a knight and I want to become one," she said firmly. "Now get a grip and tell that mopey mount of mine to buck up!"

By the third day, Posy and Sir Limpalong were jousting at full gallop with their wooden sticks. The other knightlets had bandages around their heads and patches over their eyes.

"Just because you can do that doesn't mean you'll be any good when it comes to the real thing," Sir Darren taunted.

"Why don't you show us how it's done?" Posy asked.

"If you can," Hodgepodge added.

"I couldn't possibly," Sir Darren replied, puffing out his chest.

"Please, Sir Darren," Posy asked. "It would be such a thrill."

"Well, obviously," Sir Darren said, running a finger over his arrogant eyebrows, "but I'm not going to give any of my winning tips to you lot. I'm saving those for George, even though he's a jousting genius."

Posy opened her eyes wide. In the distance, George was clinging to the top of his pole. "Mmm," Posy hummed. "It looks as if he'll make a pretty good pole-vaulter too!" Sir Darren tut-tutted very loudly and strode across the yard in a huff.

# Chapter Four

The following morning, George
received a parcel from his parents.

"I have a horrible feeling I know
what this is," he said.

"It might be an extra-long rolling
pin," Posy said hopefully.

"It's . . . " George's mouth hung
open.

"A Goodfellow family heirloom."

Posy sighed as she stroked the gilded jousting pole. "George, you are so lucky."

"I would be if I knew how to use it," George groaned. "Sir Darren struts up and down a lot, but we haven't practised properly. I think he's scared of messing up his hair. Posy, what *am* I going to do?"

"Don't worry," Posy said. "I'm sure I can use my princess powers to come up with a plan to save the day."

At lunchtime, Posy and Sir Limpalong rode outside the Knight School walls for a picnic. Sir Limpalong presented Posy with something wrapped in

brown paper. It was a jousting pole that had once been beautiful but was now rather scratched and very faded. It didn't look nearly as nice as George's.

Posy tried to look pleased.

"That," said Sir Limpalong proudly, "is my most precious pole. It's very old and a bit battered, just like me, but I want you to have it."

Posy kissed him on the cheek.

The yard was getting very crowded. Knightlets were charging in all directions, jousting poles were flying through the air and horses were ducking and weaving.

"We could do with a bit more space," Sir Limpalong said.

"Somewhere safe and quiet," Daisy agreed as a low-flying jousting pole whizzed past her fetlock.

"I know just the place," Posy said. "Follow me!"

Princess Posy led the way through the back gates of Peppermint Palace, across the cobbled yard and down the wide stone steps into the kitchen. The huge, high room had a narrow trestle table running down the middle. It was loaded with sandwiches, pastries, puddings and a tall chocolate cake.

"Are you sure it's all right to come in here?" Sir Limpalong asked anxiously. "Won't the King and Queen mind."

"They won't know," Posy said. "It's Friday, so all the staff are given the afternoon off because Mum goes to the gym and Dad's at bingo, trying to win a king's ransom."

Sir Limpalong made two marks with some royal-blue wool at either end of the room.

"What about all this food?" Sir Limpalong asked, pointing to the plates and bowls that were piled high.

"It'll be fine," Posy said. "It's probably just stuff for supper."

Posy began to practise. The jousting pole was very long and Daisy was very twitchy. As Posy flashed the pole from side to side, she whisked the tops off some jellies.

"Oops!" She giggled as a cloud of orange, red and green goo splatted in Sir Limpalong's face.

"This is a feast fit for a king," Sir Limpalong chuckled, slurping some of the jelly.

Daisy pawed at the ground and charged the length of the room. Posy aimed the pole towards the ball of wool Sir Limpalong had hung from the ceiling. She missed the target but speared a platter full of sandwiches on to her jousting pole.

"Very tasty!" Hodgepodge said, munching several slices of cucumber.

Daisy dashed down one side of the table while Hodgepodge cantered along the other. Sir Limpalong raised his walking stick in the air. Posy swizzled her jousting pole above her head.

Suddenly she lost her grip and the pole flew across the table and crashed into the chocolate cake.

"Crumbs!" Hodgepodge snorted.

"I'm such a butterfingers," Posy gasped. "Will I ever get the hang of this?"

"You won't have to worry about your

jousting technique when your parents see this mess," Daisy warned. "We'll be destined for the dungeons."

"Where have you been?" George asked Posy that evening. "I haven't seen you all day."

"Practising, of course," Posy replied. "What about you?"

"I've been making a fairy-tale-castle cake for my parents. I thought it might make them feel better when I fail to get my golden spurs," George explained.

"Hasn't Sir Darren been showing you a hundred and one daring ways to

202

defeat your opponent?" Posy asked.

"Nah," George laughed. "He reckons I don't need much tuition. He says jousting is bound to come to me as naturally as falling off a horse. I wish he was right." George sighed. "I've tried and tried but I'm a hopeless horseman even *without* a jousting pole. I'll just have to pretend I'm ill tomorrow."

"You can't do that!" Posy scolded. "Meet me in the dragons' field on the stroke of midnight. Bring your rolling pin and those long skewer things you put kebabs on."

"Are we going to have a barbecue?" George's eyes lit up.

"No we are not," Posy said sternly. "I'm going to teach you to joust if it's the last thing I do before returning to being a prissy princess."

"This seems a bit odd to me," Daisy huffed as Posy led her out of the stables just before midnight. "George is your opponent. You're not meant to be helping him."

"He's my friend too, Daisy," Posy said gently, "and I don't want him getting into trouble."

George was already waiting with Typhoon Tom.

"I'd much rather be dreaming up a

new dish than dashing around a
muddy field in the dark," he moaned.

Posy gave him a stern look and then
began to teach George to joust using a
rolling pin.

"Mind my head," Daisy instructed
him. "I don't want to get my best bridle
bashed. I need to look absolutely
flawless for Hurricane Henry."

Then Posy showed George how to
hold the kebab skewers.

"Watch what you're doing with
those," Typhoon Tom said, shuddering.
"I don't want to have to pull out of
the competition because I've been
skewered!"

Finally, as the moon dipped behind the Knight School and the sun peeped above Peppermint Palace, Posy showed George how to fight with a jousting pole.

"I think you've cracked it," she sighed as the four of them trudged back for breakfast.

"Thanks, Posy," George smiled. "At least I won't make a complete fool of myself now."

"Thanks, Posy," Daisy groaned, staring into the mirror. "I've got the biggest bags under my eyes. How am I going to hide those from Hunky Henry?"

# Chapter Five

By mid-morning the Knight School grounds were full of people waiting for the tournament to begin. Posy polished her suit of armour and fixed some feathers on to her helmet. She applied her lucky lipgloss and went to get Daisy.

Daisy was wearing Sir Limpalong's royal-blue blanket. She was having a gigantic sulk.

"You only have to wear it for a little while," Posy soothed. "Then you can take it off. Actually it quite suits you."

Posy threaded multicoloured jewels through Daisy's mane and tied a beautiful blue chiffon bow to her tail. It didn't make any difference to Daisy's mood.

"Please make an effort," Posy pleaded. "How are we going to get good marks for style if you're the unhappiest horse in the land?"

Daisy just tossed her mane stroppily, whisked her tail until the bow came undone and stomped out of the stables.

Posy and George were the last competitors to take part in the tournament.

"Uh-oh!" George groaned. "It's kick-off time."

Sir Limpalong took Posy's hand in his. "Whatever happens," he said, starting to bow, "it's been a pleasure working with you, Princess Posy."

PRINCESS POSY, KNIGHT-IN-TRAINING

"No," Posy said, straightening him up, "it's been a real honour for me to learn from such a special knight and his handsome horse." She held out a pink sugar lump for Hodgepodge.

The trumpeter trumpeted, the crowd cheered and Posy held hands tightly with George and Sir Limpalong.

"Don't worry," she smiled. "I've got a plan, just like I promised. Everything will be all right. Trust me."

Posy and George trotted out to tumultuous applause. The King put two fingers in his mouth and gave a long, loud whistle. The Queen was holding a banner that said "Power to the

Princess". Next to them sat the
Goodfellows, looking very proud.

"What's this plan?" Daisy asked
grumpily as she positioned herself at
one end of the tournament ground.

Posy leaned forwards and whispered the secret in her horse's ear.

"Harrumph!" Daisy neighed rudely.

"I know, I know," Posy snapped, "but it's the best I can come up with on the spur of the moment."

The King held up the starting flag and Posy gave the thumbs-up sign to George.

"Here goes," Posy whispered to Daisy. "Not too fast to start with. Give George time to settle Typhoon Tom."

Posy and George cantered slowly towards each other. Posy aimed her jousting pole at George's shield and tapped it as lightly as she could. The

shield spun in George's hand and
Typhoon Tom reared magnificently, but
George stayed in the saddle.

"Phew!" Posy breathed.

They turned. George pointed his
jousting pole at Posy. She leaned slightly
to the right and there was a thud as the
pole made contact with her breastplate.

Posy jerked backwards and saw the
umpire mark one point each on the
blackboard. Sir Darren Daring clapped
loudly from the sidelines.

"Here goes, Daisy," Posy gulped as
she urged her horse forwards. "This is
the deciding run. Remember what I
told you."

Daisy got off to a flying start. Typhoon Tom was galloping at full speed.

Posy raised her pole. It clashed violently against George's.

Typhoon Tom spun in a circle. George couldn't hold on. He crashed to the ground. The audience gasped and groaned, but Daisy quickly bucked and hoofed great clouds of dust into the air with an extra large blast towards Sir Darren.

The audience coughed and blinked through the billowing haze. For a split second nobody could see a thing. Princess Posy slid to the ground and

arranged herself artistically next to George.

"Don't move," she instructed. "Let's just wait for the dust to settle!"

# Chapter Six

"I got a real kick out of that," Daisy
said, nuzzling Posy's cheek.
"Especially blasting Sir Darren
Dreadful!"

"He's hopping mad!" Posy giggled,
looking over to where Sir Darren was
leaping from one foot to the other
and shouting, while all the other
knights tried to dust him down with

their banners. Sir Limpalong hobbled over and helped Posy up. He looked a teeny-weeny bit cross too.

"You could have blown it," he whispered to Posy.

"I'm sorry," she said. "What else could I do?"

Sir Limpalong put his arm around her.

"Nothing," he said. "You did the honourable thing."

Posy held her breath as the steward raised a loudhailer to his lips.

"The contest between George Goodfellow and Princess Posy is a draw," he announced. "Both will be awarded their golden spurs."

"Try to look pleased," Posy said as she hugged George.

"I am," he replied. "Thanks, Posy.

My parents will be so thrilled."

"Ahem!" The King stepped forwards. "Tea will be served on the Peppermint Palace terrace. Unfortunately, due to an upset in the kitchen yesterday, the usual tournament cake will not be displayed or, er, eaten."

There were groans from the crowd.

"George!" Posy nudged. "This is your chance to *really* impress your parents. Go and get that cake you made for them."

★

Sir Darren Daring strutted and bowed and patted himself on the back as George collected his golden spurs.

"Even the best knights take a tumble sometimes," he fawned in front of the King. "Of course, if it hadn't been for my terrific tuition it could have been much worse."

When it was Posy's turn, Sir Darren managed a shifty smirk.

"I don't know how a knitting knight and a persistent princess made it to the finish," he snarled.

"If it makes you any happier," Sir Limpalong said, fixing Posy's spurs to her boots, "we did turn to jelly at one point!"

"SILENCE!" the King boomed. "I have one more announcement to make."

He beckoned to Sir Limpalong to join him on the platform.

"Looks like the old boy's collecting his pension scroll," Sir Darren sniggered at Posy. "Not before time either."

Posy glared at Sir Darren, but she felt tears pricking behind her eyes. Surely her father couldn't force Sir Limpalong to retire . . .

"It has come to my royal notice," the King said, "that several of our Knights of the Realm are in need of a refresher course." The King clasped Sir Limpalong's hand and lifted his arm

high into the air. The joints in his freshly oiled armour moved smoothly and silently.

"Hear! hear!" Sir Darren cheered. "Standards must not be allowed to slip."

The King looked at Posy and winked. Then he gazed at Sir Darren.

"I'm glad you agree," he said, "because I have decided to appoint Sir Limpalong to a very special position in honour of his years of devoted service."

Sir Darren gulped. His awesome jaw started to quiver. The crowd was so still that Posy thought they must have been put under a magic spell.

"This wisest of knights," the King beamed, "is to be an elite tutor. And you, Sir Darren Daring, have been chosen to be his first pupil."

Sir Darren was speechless. Sir Limpalong went pink with pride. Posy and George clapped louder than anyone as Sir Darren was pushed up on to the stage and forced to shake hands with Sir Limpalong.

"That," Posy laughed as she cut herself a large piece of George's cake with her sword, "really is the icing on the cake!"

"We did it, Daisy," Posy giggled as she pinned a gold rosette to her horse's bridle. "At last I'm a proper Knight of the Realm."

"Your parents looked prouder than the palace peacocks," Daisy neighed.

"And George's parents are so impressed by his cooking," Posy added, "they've agreed to him being a part-time knight so he can train as a chef as well."

"Hodgepodge won't have to be put out to grass," Daisy sighed thankfully.

"And Hurricane Henry seems to have fallen head over hoofs in love with you as a result of Sir Limpalong's knitting," Posy teased.

"He said the colour blue brings out the beauty of my eyes." Daisy blushed. "It's all ended well."

"Oh no, Daisy," Posy giggled, hugging her horse tightly. "That's the best bit. This isn't the end. It's only the beginning."

## ALEX GUTTERIDGE

## Rules the Waves

*Meet Polly — she's a pretty perfect pirate!*

Seafaring scoundrels Mad-Eyed Mick, Stinky Dave and Press-Gang Pete are always on the lookout for ways to wreck Polly's plans to be a proper pirate.

Can she tackle the troublemaking trio and still come top at treasure hunting?

*Three shiver-yer-timbers tales in one barnacle-busting book!*

**ALEX GUTTERIDGE**

# Witch Wendy
## Works her Magic

*Meet Wendy – she'll put a spell on you!*

Witch Wendy gets muddled by magic, troubled by tricks and
flying puts her in a flap. She just can't get anything right!

Luckily her clever cat, Snowflake, is always ready to lend a
helping paw and make sure everything turns out purrrfectly.

*Three enchanting tales in one magical book!*

# A selected list of titles available from Macmillan Children's Books

The prices shown below are correct at the time of going to press. However, Macmillan Publishers reserves the right to show new retail prices on covers, which may differ from those previously advertised.